I AM READING

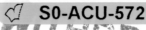
SO-ACU-572

WITHDRAWN

MR. COOL

JACQUELINE WILSON

ILLUSTRATED BY
STEPHEN LEWIS

Livonia Public Library
CARL SANDBURG BRANCH #21
30100 W. 7 Mile Road
Livonia, Mich. 48152
248-893-4010

KINGFISHER
BOSTON

J READER

3 9082 09450 2724

KINGFISHER
a Houghton Mifflin Company imprint
222 Berkeley Street
Boston, Massachusetts 02116
www.houghtonmifflinbooks.com

First published by Kingfisher in 1996
This edition published in 2004
2 4 6 8 10 9 7 5 3 1
1TR/0104/TWP/GRS(GRS)/115SEM

Text copyright © Jacqueline Wilson 1996
Illustrations copyright © Stephen Lewis 1996

All rights reserved under International
and Pan-American Copyright Conventions

LIBRARY OF CONGRESS CATALOGING–IN–PUBLICATION DATA
has been applied for.

ISBN 0-7534-5822-5

Printed in India

Livonia Public Library
CARL SANDBURG BRANCH #21
30100 W. 7 Mile Road
Livonia, Mich. 48152
248-893-4010

Contents

Chapter One

Ricky wanted to be a rock star.

He was excellent at singing.

He was excellent at dancing.

He looked excellent too.

Ricky had floppy, fair hair

that fell into his blue eyes.

Ricky always wore blue jeans.

Ricky looked cool.

Micky wanted to be a rock star.

He was terrific at singing.

He was terrific at dancing.

He looked terrific too.

Micky had long, red hair
and wicked green eyes.

Micky always wore black.

Micky looked cool.

Nicky wanted to be a rock star.

He was fantastic at singing.

He was fantastic at dancing.

He looked fantastic too.

Nicky had curly, black hair

and big brown eyes.

Nicky always wore leather.

Nicky looked cool.

Kevin wanted to be a rock star.

He wasn't great at singing.

He wasn't great at dancing.

He didn't look great either.

Kevin had straight, mousy hair
and gray eyes.

Kevin always wore a sweater,
knitted by his grandma, and sweatpants.

Kevin didn't look cool.

But he had a great smile.

Ricky and Micky and Nicky
formed a band.

"Can I be in the band too?"
asked Kevin.

Ricky and Micky and Nicky
weren't sure.

"You're a nice guy, Kevin.
But you're not that great at singing,"
said Ricky.

Kevin smiled bravely.

Ricky felt bad.

"We do like you, Kevin.
But you're not that great at dancing,"
said Micky.

Kevin smiled bravely.

Micky felt bad.

"You can't help it, Kevin.
You just don't look cool,"
said Nicky.
Kevin smiled bravely.
Nicky felt bad.

9

"I wish I could be in your band,"

said Kevin, still smiling.

"Come on, you guys.

Let me be in the band.

I'll try hard at singing.

I'll try hard at dancing.

I'll try hard to look cool."

Ricky and Micky and Nicky

still weren't sure.

"My grandma has a basement," said Kevin.

"We could practice there.

My grandma won't mind."

Ricky and Micky and Nicky

didn't have a good place to practice.

Ricky lived in a small house.

Ricky's mom and dad

griped and grumbled

when the boys in the band

started playing.

Micky lived in a house with a lot of pets.
All the pets howled and yowled
when the boys in the band
started playing.

Nicky lived in an apartment.

Nicky's neighbors came to his door

and huffed and puffed

when the boys in the band

started playing.

"Can we practice in your grandma's basement anytime?" Ricky asked Kevin.

"You bet," said Kevin.

"Right," said Ricky. "You can be in the band then, Kevin. Okay, Micky?"

"Okay with me," said Micky.

"Okay, Nicky?"

"Okay with me," said Nicky.

"You're one of the band,

now, Kevin," said Ricky.

"G–r–e–a–t!" said Kevin,

and he smiled and smiled and smiled.

Chapter Two

Ricky and Micky and Nicky and Kevin

practiced every night

in Kevin's grandma's basement.

Kevin's grandma brought them drinks

and chocolate-chip cookies.

The band practiced
and practiced
and practiced.
Ricky and Micky and Nicky
got even better at singing.
Kevin still wasn't that great at singing.

Ricky and Micky and Nicky

got even better at dancing.

Kevin still wasn't that great at dancing.

Ricky and Micky and Nicky
all looked supercool.

Kevin didn't look cool at all.

But Ricky and Micky and Nicky
didn't want to push Kevin
out of the band.

They liked Kevin.

And they needed to practice

in Kevin's grandma's basement.

It was Kevin's grandma

who got the boys their first gig.

"My friend goes to this club.

They want a band for Saturday night.

I said I know a very good band.

Okay with you, boys?" said Kevin's grandma.

"Okay with me!" said Ricky.

"Okay with me!" said Micky.

"Okay with me!" said Nicky.

"G–r–e–a–t!" said Kevin.

"Thanks, Grandma!"

The band practiced even harder
for their Saturday night gig.

"What should we call our band?"
said Ricky.

"How about Ricky and Micky
and Nicky and Kevin?"
said Kevin.

"That doesn't sound very cool, Kevin,"
said Ricky.

"I'm not a very cool guy,"
said Kevin.

"Not like you, Ricky.
You're a real Mr. Cool.
And you, Micky.
You're a real Mr. Cool too.
And you, Nicky.
Yet another
Mr. Cool."

"Mr. Cool," said Ricky.

He snapped his fingers.

"Excellent name!"

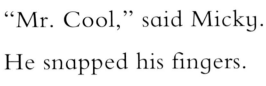

"Mr. Cool," said Micky.

He snapped his fingers.

"Terrific name!"

"Mr. Cool," said Nicky.

He snapped his fingers.

"Fantastic name!"

"Mr. Cool," said Kevin.

He tried to snap his fingers,

but they got stuck.

It didn't matter.

"G–r–e–a–t,"

said Kevin,

and he smiled

and smiled

and smiled.

So the boys called the band Mr. Cool.

They didn't feel very cool

just before their first gig.

Ricky had problems with his voice.

Micky had problems with his feet.

Nicky had problems with his hair.

Kevin had lots and lots
and lots of problems.
"We're awful,"
said Ricky, Micky, and Nicky.
"We can't go on."
"I'm awful," said Kevin.
"But you guys are
excellent,
terrific,
fantastic.
We're going on.
And we're going
to be great."

So Mr. Cool played their first gig.

They were great.

Ricky and Micky and Nicky were excellent at singing.

Ricky and Micky and Nicky were terrific at dancing.

Ricky and Micky and Nicky looked fantastic.

Kevin still wasn't great at singing.

Or dancing.

Kevin still didn't look great either.

But he had a great smile.

And all the people in the club smiled too.

They clapped and cheered

when the band took a bow.

Mr. Cool was a big success.

Chapter Three

Ricky and Micky and Nicky and Kevin

played at the club every Saturday night.

They were asked to play

at a lot of other clubs too.

And school dances.

And cafés.

They even did a gig at a birthday party,
but that was just for Kevin's grandma.

Then one night a man named Mr. Rich
came to hear the boys play.
Mr. Rich was well-known
in the music world.

The boys were very nervous

when they spotted Mr. Rich.

"Don't worry, guys," said Kevin.

"We'll be great."

Kevin smiled,

and Ricky and Micky and Nicky

smiled back.

They did their act in front of Mr. Rich.

Ricky and Micky and Nicky

were excellent at singing.

Ricky and Micky and Nicky

were terrific at dancing.

Ricky and Micky and Nicky

looked fantastic too.

Kevin wasn't great at singing.

Kevin wasn't great at dancing.

Kevin didn't look great either,

despite his new hand-knit sweater.

"You boys are incredible," said Mr. Rich.

"You're a great band.

I want to sign you up.

Well . . . I want three of you."

He pointed at Ricky.

He pointed at Micky.

He pointed at Nicky.

He didn't point at Kevin.

He shook his head.

"Sorry, kid," said Mr. Rich to Kevin.

"I don't want you in the band."

Kevin stopped smiling.

He nodded sadly and walked away.

"Hang on, Kevin!" said Ricky.

"You're part of Mr. Cool.

I say you take all four of us, Mr. Rich

—or none of us.

Okay with you, boys?"

"Okay with me!" said Micky.

"Okay with me!" said Nicky.

Kevin didn't say anything.

But he smiled.

"Okay with me, too,"

said Mr. Rich, sighing.

Mr. Rich groomed the boys for stardom.

They made their first album.

Ricky and Micky and Nicky

were excellent at singing

on their first Mr. Cool album.

Kevin wasn't that great.

He sang very softly.

They made their first video.

Ricky and Micky and Nicky

were terrific at dancing

on their first Mr. Cool video.

Kevin wasn't that great.

He danced out of camera shot

most of the time.

They posed for their first

Mr. Cool photo shoot.

Ricky and Micky and Nicky

looked fantastic,

really supercool.

Kevin didn't look great.

He stood behind the other boys.

Mr. Rich set up a big concert tour
for Mr. Cool.

Ricky and Micky and Nicky
were *so* nervous.

Even Mr. Rich was a little bit nervous.

But Kevin told them not to worry.

"Stay cool, you guys," he said.

"They'll think we're great, you'll see."

All the girls and boys did think
Mr. Cool was a great band.
They thought they were
excellent, terrific,
fantastic. Ricky and Micky
and Nicky and Kevin sang.
Ricky and Micky and Nicky
and Kevin danced.
Ricky and Micky
and Nicky and Kevin posed
in their new stage outfits.
Kevin chatted
to the audience.
"Hope you're having
a great time," he said,
and he smiled.

He saw his grandma at the back.

He waved.

Grandma waved back.

And all the girls and boys waved too.

"We're having a great time, Kevin,"

they yelled.

"We love Mr. Cool.

We love Ricky.

We love Micky.

We love Nicky.

And most of all—we love you, Kevin!

We think you're g-r-e-a-t!"

Kevin smiled and smiled and smiled.

About the author and illustrator

Jacqueline Wilson has written many books for children, including *Double Act,* which won the Smarties Book Prize in the U.K. Jacqueline says, "Kevin certainly doesn't look cool like the rest of the boys in the band—but he's so funny and friendly it doesn't matter a bit."

Stephen Lewis graduated from art school in 1994 and has been illustrating children's books ever since. "I went to school with some guys who formed a band," says Stephen. "They became just as successful as Mr. Cool—but none of them was like Kevin."

Strategies for Beginner Readers

Predict
Think about the cover, illustrations, and the title of the book. What do you think this book will be about? While you are reading think about what may happen next and why.

Monitor
As you read ask yourself if what you're reading makes sense. If it doesn't, reread, look at the illustrations, or read ahead.

Question
Ask yourself questions about important ideas in the story such as what the characters might do or what you might learn.

Phonics
If there is a word that you do not know, look carefully at the letters, sounds, and word parts that you do know. Blend the sounds to read the word. Ask yourself if this is a word you know. Does it make sense in the sentence?

Summarize
Think about the characters, the setting where the story takes place, and the problem the characters faced in the story. Tell the important ideas in the beginning, middle, and end of the story.

Evaluate
Ask yourself questions like: Did you like the story? Why or why not? How did the author make the story come alive? How did the author make the story fun to read? How well did you understand the story? Maybe you can understand it better if you read it again!